Penguin  Readers

WHAT YOU ARE LOOKING FOR IS IN THE LIBRARY

MICHIKO AOYAMA

LEVEL

RETOLD BY KIRSTY LOEHR
ILLUSTRATED BY ROHAN EASON
SERIES EDITOR: SORREL PITTS

⚠ Contains adult content, which could include: sexual behaviour or exploitation, misuse of alcohol, smoking, illegal drugs, violence and dangerous behaviour.

PENGUIN BOOKS

UK | USA | Canada | Ireland | Australia
India | New Zealand | South Africa

Penguin Books is part of the Penguin Random House group of companies whose addresses can be found at global.penguinrandomhouse.com.
www.penguin.co.uk www.puffin.co.uk www.ladybird.co.uk

First published in Japan as お探し物は図書室まで by POPLAR Publishing Co., Ltd 2020
First published in English in Great Britain as *What You Are Looking For Is In The Library* by Doubleday, an imprint of Transworld Publishers 2023
This Penguin Readers edition published by Penguin Books Ltd 2026
001

Original text written by Michiko Aoyama
Text for Penguin Readers edition adapted by Kirsty Loehr
Original copyright © Michiko Aoyama 2020
Text for Penguin Readers edition copyright © Penguin Books Ltd, 2026
Illustrated by Rohan Eason
Illustrations copyright © Penguin Books Ltd, 2023, 2026
Cover image design and illustration © Anna Morrison
Art direction by Marianne Issa El-Khoury/TW

The moral right of the original author and the original illustrator has been asserted

Penguin Random House values and supports copyright. Copyright fuels creativity, encourages diverse voices, promotes freedom of expression and supports a vibrant culture. Thank you for purchasing an authorized edition of this book and for respecting intellectual property laws by not reproducing, scanning or distributing any part of it by any means without permission. You are supporting authors and enabling Penguin Random House to continue to publish books for everyone. No part of this book may be used or reproduced in any manner for the purpose of training artificial intelligence technologies or systems. In accordance with Article 4(3) of the DSM Directive 2019/790, Penguin Random House expressly reserves this work from the text and data mining exception.

Printed and bound in Great Britain by Clays Ltd, Elcograf S.p.A.

The authorized representative in the EEA is Penguin Random House Ireland, Morrison Chambers, 32 Nassau Street, Dublin D02 YH68

A CIP catalogue record for this book is available from the British Library

ISBN: 978–0–241–75396–5

All correspondence to:
Penguin Books
Penguin Random House Children's
One Embassy Gardens, 8 Viaduct Gardens,
London SW11 7BW

Penguin Random House is committed to a sustainable future for our business, our readers and our planet. This book is made from Forest Stewardship Council® certified paper.

Contents

People in the story	4
New words	5
Note about the story	6
Before-reading questions	6
Chapter One – Tomoka Fujiki, 21, shop worker	7
Chapter Two – Ryo Urase, 35, accountant	18
Chapter Three – Natsumi Sakitani, 40, works in publishing	33
Chapter Four – Hiroya Suda, 30, not working	45
Chapter Five – Masao Gonno, 65, retired	56
During-reading questions	70
After-reading questions	72
Exercises	73
Project work	76
Glossary	77

People in the story

Tomoka Fujiki

Sayuri Komachi

Ryo Urase

Natsumi Sakitani

Hiroya Suda

Masao Gonno

New words

crab

felting

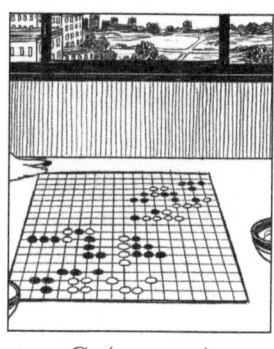

Go (a game)

laptop

mice

worm

Note about the story

What You Are Looking For Is In The Library is by the Japanese writer Michiko Aoyama. In her story, the **librarian*** Sayuri Komachi is a very interesting and strange person who **recommends** books to help people find what they are *really* looking for in life. The books are special for each person. They show them life is not always how you want it to be, but it is still good. The librarian also gives each person a **felted** gift that she has made. The felted gifts all mean something to the visitors, but they don't understand why until later. Both the books and the felted gifts help each person understand their place in the world.

Michiko Aoyama visited libraries to escape real life. She wanted to show that we don't always choose books but that sometimes they choose us. She loves reading and, like Hiroya in the book, she is interested in Japanese **manga**. Manga is Japanese drawing that is used for telling stories to children, young people and adults. It is used in many Japanese **magazines**.

Before-reading questions

1 Why do people go to libraries, do you think?

2 This story happens in Japan. Are you from Japan? Have you visited Japan?

3 In the story, librarian Sayuri Komachi makes people gifts. Have you ever made someone a gift? What was it and why?

*Definitions of words in **bold** can be found in the glossary on pages 77–79.

CHAPTER ONE
Tomoka Fujiki, 21, shop worker

Saya sends me a message telling me that she has a new boyfriend.

What's he like? I write back.

He's a doctor, she replies.

She doesn't tell me what he looks like or give any more information about his job. I know what a doctor is, and a job tells you a little about someone's **personality**—but only a little. Then I start thinking about my own job. What does it say about *my* personality?

I've known Saya since high school. When I left home and moved to Tokyo, we stayed friends. She messages me again and asks me how I am.

Great! I write.

I really mean *bored*.

I work at a big store called Eden. Every morning, I put on my black skirt and orange shirt. Then I spend the day standing around and helping **customers**. I started this job six months ago after finishing college.

"Miss Fujiki," says Mrs. Numauchi, "I've had my lunch. You can go next."

Mrs. Numauchi also works at Eden. She's worked here for a long time. Last month was her birthday, and I think she is about my mother's age. Mrs. Numauchi tells me what to do a lot of the time, but she is usually right.

I walk toward the **staff** restaurant. The woman who

works there doesn't like me because one time she made a mistake with my order. So, I don't buy my lunch from the restaurant any more—I buy a sandwich from the store on the way to work and eat it there. I don't know how to cook, so I usually buy cheap food that is ready to eat.

I can hear some of my **colleagues** in the restaurant talking about their husbands and children. To a customer, I am just like my colleagues, wearing the same orange shirt. But I'm not like them, and I usually try to stay away from them. I don't like working here but it was the only place that gave me a job. Eden is also in Tokyo, and I don't want to go back to the countryside where there is just rice field after rice field and only one store. Tokyo has always been my dream city, and I still love it, but what about the future?

When I lived in the countryside, people thought it was wonderful that I was moving to Tokyo. They thought that I was great. Saya still thinks it's good that I live here and that I have a great job. I won't tell her that I only work in a clothes shop. I'm **embarrassed**. I'm not great, and I have no **ambition** to *be* great. I don't even have a boyfriend. I worry that I'll be at Eden until I'm my mother's age, like Mrs. Numauchi.

"Hey, Tomoka," calls Kiriyama. He works at the glasses shop. He is around the same age as me and the only person I can talk to. "Is it OK if I join you for lunch?" he asks while carrying some food.

"Sure," I say.

Kiriyama sits down in front of me. He is wearing a nice

pair of glasses that look really good on his face. You can see that he is great at his job. "Hey, what did you do before working here?" I ask.

"I worked for a **magazine**," he says.

"Really? I didn't know you worked in **publishing**," I say.

"Are you surprised?" he asks.

"You had a great job but then you came here," I say.

Kiriyama smiles. "Working in a glasses shop is also great."

"I will work for Eden until I die," I say, sadly.

"Do you want to change jobs?"

"Yeah," I say.

"Do you still want to work with customers?" he asks.

"Yeah. But I would prefer to work in an office. I also want to wear what I like and go outside to a café for lunch with my colleagues. How did you find this job?" I ask.

"I looked on a website for people who want to change jobs," he said.

Kiriyama pulls out his smartphone and shows me the website.

"You complete the information about your **skills** and then they find you a job that needs the same ones. Look, here are some of the skills that people want," he says, pointing at the website.

I don't have all the computer skills that are on the website—I can use Word but not Excel or PowerPoint. I have a laptop, but I never use it.

"If you want to work in an office, you need to know Excel," Kiriyama says. "Why don't you take a class to learn how to use it?"

"Computer classes are expensive," I say.

"Libraries often have cheap classes," Kiriyama tells me.

"Really? I didn't know," I say.

When I get home, I look on my phone for the nearest

library. I find Hatori Library, which is ten minutes from my apartment. It has classes on writing, math, and other skills. I can't believe that I didn't know about this. The computer class isn't too expensive, and it's every Wednesday afternoon. For the first time in a long while, I feel a little excited about something.

Two days later, I'm standing inside the library with my laptop. I find my class and introduce myself to the teacher, Ms. Gonno.

"Hello, my name is Tomoka," I say.

Ms. Gonno gives me a friendly smile and tells me to sit down. For the next two hours, I learn all about Excel. I've been in my apartment doing nothing all this time, not far from this library. The more I think about it, the worse it makes me feel.

"Do you want to borrow any books?" Ms. Gonno says when the class finishes.

"I can borrow books?" I say, surprised.

"Yes, anybody who lives near the library can borrow six books for two weeks," she says, smiling.

I look at the rows of books and see a small girl putting some onto a shelf.

"Excuse me, where are the books on computers?" I ask. The girl looks young enough to still be in high school.

"Over here," she says.

She walks past a large reading table and points to a shelf on the wall.

"My name is Nozomi Morinaga. If you need any

recommendations, the **librarian** is in the office. She knows more than I do."

"Recommendations?" I ask.

"You can tell her what you're looking for, and she will give you recommendations," Nozomi says. "Her name is Sayuri Komachi."

"Thanks," I say.

I walk to the office room and look inside. Wow! Sayuri Komachi is huge—not fat, but just very big. You can't see where her head ends, and her neck begins. Her skin is also really white. She is looking down at something, but I can't see what she is looking at. I move closer and see that she is **felting** with a **needle**.

"What are you looking for?" she says, turning toward me.

Her voice is strange but warm.

"I'm looking for books about how to use a computer," I say.

I notice an orange box on her desk. It is a box of Honeydome cookies by Kuremiyado. The librarian opens the box but inside are some felting needles. Ms. Komachi puts away her needle, and then looks at me.

"What do you want to do on the computer?" she replies.

"Excel, to begin with," I say. "I want to learn some computer skills, and then I can change my job."

"What do you do?" she asks.

"Nothing great," I say.

"Don't you like your job?"

"It's not my dream job, and anybody can do it," I say.

TOMOKA FUJIKI, 21, SHOP WORKER

"But I live alone, and I need to work."

"You found a job, you go to work every day, and you feed yourself. I think that's excellent," she says.

Nobody has ever said that about me before. It's like she can see the real me. I want to cry.

Ms. Komachi turns to the computer, begins **typing**, and

then hands me a **list** of books. I look at the list and see that all but one are about computer skills. The other one is *Guri and Gura*, a children's book about two mice. She then reaches below the desk and pulls out a soft and colorful felted **frying pan**.

"What's this?" I ask.

"A gift," she says.

"Did you make this?"

"Yes," she says.

Ms. Komachi turns back to her needles and starts felting again. I don't think she wants to talk to me any more, so I put the frying pan into my **pocket**, and walk away.

I find the **recommended** books and choose two that seem easy to understand. But what about *Guri and Gura*? Maybe I should get that, too. I read it many times when I was a child. Why did Ms. Komachi recommend it? I go to the children's part and find it, then I take my books to Nozomi.

I go home and look at *Guri and Gura* and read the story from the pictures. In the story, Guri and Gura find a huge egg, and they don't know what to do with it. Then, they decide to make a cake called *castella*. Toward the end of the book is a picture of the big frying pan that they use. I remember the frying pan that Ms. Komachi gave me.

I read the book again. *Egg, sugar, and milk. They mix it and cook it in the frying pan.*

I didn't know that *castella* was so easy to make.

The next day, I see Kiriyama at lunchtime.

TOMOKA FUJIKI, 21, SHOP WORKER

"Do you want a rice ball?" he says. "I made them myself."
"Do you cook?" I ask.
"I do now," Kiriyama says.
"This rice ball is great," I say, eating one.
"Eating is important," he tells me. "Work hard and eat well."
"Kiriyama, why did you **quit** your job at the magazine?"
He starts eating another rice ball. "There were only a few of us working there, and we had a lot to do. Sometimes we worked all night, and we were very tired. Our **manager** didn't care about us, and he always gave us more work to do. I thought working that hard was normal, but I was wrong. I had no time to cook, and I sometimes slept on the office floor. I was working to eat, but I never had time to eat well," he says.
"I didn't know that working for a magazine was so difficult," I say.
"Not every place is like that," he says. "There are also people who like working that hard. It just wasn't me."
After lunch, I think about cooking something, too, but I can't decide what to make. I think about the frying pan again that Ms. Komachi gave to me. I know what I'll make: *castella*, just like in *Guri and Gura*. I look on my smartphone and type in *Guri and Gura castella*. So many people have tried to make the same cake from the **recipe** in the book. I follow the recipe and start making it. I'm making *castella*! I put everything into a real frying pan and wash my hands. Then, I look at myself in the mirror. My skin is bad,

WHAT YOU ARE LOOKING FOR IS IN THE LIBRARY

and I look tired. My apartment is so dirty, and there are clothes everywhere.

Like Kiriyama, I have forgotten how to look after myself, so I clean the apartment while the cake cooks. It smells so nice. When I'm finished, I check on the cake, but the bottom is burned. What did I do wrong? I suddenly start laughing. I won't quit! I *can* learn how to make this cake.

Every day after work, I try to make the same cake. I look **online** for new recipes, but I keep getting it wrong. Then, one day I get it right.

"Wow, this is great!" Kiriyama says the next day when he tries it.

I spend so much time in the kitchen, I begin to cook dinner as well. It's amazing how much more energy I have and how much healthier I feel after only a few days.

When I return the books to Nozomi, I go and see Ms. Komachi. As I stand in front of her, she stops and looks up at me.

"Thank you," I say. "For *Guri and Gura*, and the frying pan. I learned something important."

"I did nothing," Ms. Komachi replies. "You took what you needed and did it yourself."

I still don't know what I want to do, or what I can do. But it's OK. Now I know that I don't have to worry. I'm just happy learning some new skills and living my life. Because I never know when I might find my own huge egg.

CHAPTER TWO
Ryo Urase, 35, accountant

It all began with a spoon that I took from a shelf. It was very small and flat and looked like a teaspoon. I was in high school at the time. I was walking around the streets of Kanagawa because I didn't want to go home after a small fight with my mother. That's when I found the shop, which was full of strange, old things—it was an antique shop.

I continued looking around the shop with the spoon in my hand. It was warm from holding it. After a few minutes, I bought it for 1,500 yen. That was a lot of money for a student in high school, but I didn't want to put the spoon back on the shelf.

The manager was an older man who always wore a hat. He was like an antique himself. "It's a spoon made in England," he told me.

"When was it made?" I asked.

He put on his glasses and looked at the back of the spoon. "In 1905," he said.

When I looked for myself, all I could see were letters and pictures—there were no numbers.

"How do you know?" I asked.

The manager laughed and smiled, but he didn't answer.

After that, I often visited the antique shop. The manager's name was Mr. Ebigawa, and his shop was a place where I could forget everything. Usually, I only looked, but

RYO URASE, 35, ACCOUNTANT

sometimes I bought small things. Mr. Ebigawa and the other customers taught me about antiques and how to read all the different letters and pictures. I learned so much, and I fell in love with the antique world.

Then one day, not long before I finished high school, I saw a sign on the door.

Store closed. It was the end of the antique shop and Mr. Ebigawa.

That was eighteen years ago. Maybe that's why I've always wanted my own antique shop. Even now at thirty-five, I still dream of it. When I have enough money, I will quit my job and find somewhere to open a shop. But will this day ever come?

After university, I left home and started working for a small business. I was an accountant—I helped them look after their money.

"How do you do this again?" my manager, Mr. Taguchi, asks.

"Not again," I think. He asked the same thing yesterday. Mr. Taguchi often finds things difficult to understand so I have to help him.

"That's how it's done!" he shouts. "Thanks for helping me again!"

I go back to my desk. I like working with numbers, and the job is not that difficult.

"How about a drink tomorrow?" Mr. Taguchi calls out.

"Sorry, but I'm not here tomorrow," I say.

"Are you going out with your girlfriend?" he asks.

"Yes," I say.

"Ha, I knew it." He laughs.

I'm angry at myself for telling him that I have plans to see her. Mr. Taguchi looks at me and smiles.

"You've been with this girl for a while now. Are you going to get married soon?"

"Oh no!" I say, changing the conversation. "Someone has made a mistake with the numbers. I'll need to change them."

Mr. Taguchi laughs and turns back to his computer.

I am happy that Mr. Taguchi isn't talking to me any more, but it was true that the numbers were wrong. This is my job. I have a manager who doesn't know how to do anything and colleagues who do their work badly. It's not that bad, but at times like this I want to quit. My dream is to open my own antique shop. I just want to talk to people who love antiques as much as I do. But I can't quit. I don't have enough money.

The next day, I go to pick up Hina. Hina is my girlfriend, and she lives at home with her parents.

Hina's mother opens the door. "Ryo, we haven't seen you for a while. Do you want to stay for dinner?"

Before I can answer, Hina runs out the door. "Mom, enough. Stop talking."

She takes my hand and waves to her mother.

There are ten years between Hina and me. She's only twenty-five. We met three years ago while I was walking on

Yuigahama beach at Kamakura. Hina was sitting on the sand, looking for something.

"Is everything OK?" I asked.

"I'm looking for small bits of sea-glass," she said. "I make things with it. The glass comes from something bigger that was used by somebody in another place a long time ago. I love that."

"She sees the world the same way I do," I thought.

We talked for a while, and then I asked her to have tea with me. It wasn't normal for me to ask a girl out — I still can't believe that I did it.

We share a love of old things, and sometimes Hina and

I talk about having our own shop one day, but it's just a dream. She doesn't have to worry about money because she lives at home. I have a lot more things to worry about.

Hina wants to start selling the things that she makes with sea-glass, so today we're going to the library. She has found a class there that teaches people how to build websites for businesses. While I'm waiting for Hina, I see a young girl moving some books on the shelves.

"Excuse me, do you have anything about starting a business?" I ask.

"Maybe?" she says, unsure.

"Oh, don't worry about it," I say, waving my hand and feeling bad.

"No, I'm sorry. I'm still training," she says. "My name is Nozomi Morinaga, but there's a librarian in the office who can help you."

Nozomi points toward the office so I walk over to it. When I enter, I look twice because the woman behind the desk is large. And I mean *very* large. You cannot see her neck between her head and her body.

I walk toward her slowly. She looks a little unfriendly. When I look at her hands, I notice that they are doing something behind the desk. Is she felting maybe? Yes, she is holding felting needles. I think about leaving, but then the librarian turns her head and looks at me.

"What are you looking for?" she says, and her voice is surprisingly soft.

What are you looking for? she asked me. I think about it, but

I only have dreams that will never come true. I read on her desk that her name is Sayuri Komachi.

"Do you have any books about starting a business?" I say, quietly.

"Starting a business?" she says.

"And also some advice about how to quit my job?" I ask.

Of course, I'll never start a business or quit my job.

Ms. Komachi puts her felting needles into an orange box, which I notice is a Honeydome cookie box made by Kuremiyado. I loved those cookies as a child.

"There are many different businesses. What is it that you want to do?" she asks.

"I want to own an antique shop one day," I say without thinking.

"One day?" she says.

"Well, I can't quit my job," I say, suddenly a little embarrassed. "And opening a shop will be expensive. But the more I say 'one day', the more it just sounds like a dream."

"Is that what you think?" she asks. "That it's just a dream? If you continue to say the words 'one day' then the dream isn't finished. Maybe it'll stay a beautiful dream, but the days are better when you have something to dream about."

I don't know what to say. If "one day" are the words for a dream, then what words make it real?

"But if you need to know what happens after the dream, you need to know," says Ms. Komachi. Suddenly, she turns to her computer screen and starts typing very quickly. She then hands me a list of books.

You Can Open a Store.

My Store.

Seven Things That You Should Do Before Quitting Your Job.

How Do Worms Work?

I'm sure that the last one is a mistake, so I read the name back to her. She doesn't reply but reaches into her desk and pulls out a felted brown cat.

"This is for you," she says.

"Why are you giving me this?" I ask.

"It's a free gift," she says. "Oh, and one more thing. When you go, don't forget to look at the **leaflets** near the front door. They can be very interesting."

I take the list and find the books, checking numbers and names. When Hina finds me, I'm still holding the cat.

"What's this?" Hina says.

"Something that the librarian gave me," I say.

"Are you borrowing those books?" Hina asks.

"Oh no, I was just looking," I say, a little embarrassed.

"Excuse me?" Hina calls toward Nozomi. "Can anybody borrow books?"

"Yes," Nozomi says. "Anybody who lives in this area can borrow six books for two weeks."

Hina begins talking to Nozomi, so I quickly return the business books to the shelves. Then, I take the book about worms and give it to Hina to borrow.

Before we leave, I think about Ms. Komachi and what she said about the leaflets. I look around and notice a leaflet with a photograph of a cat on the front. The cat looks like the cat that Ms. Komachi gave me. There is a man holding the cat in his arms, standing against some bookshelves. I pick up the leaflet. It says *Librarian Sayuri Komachi's favorite bookshop is* Cats Now Books—*a bookshop with real cats inside.*

"Are you coming, Ryo?" Hina says.

I put the leaflet inside the worms book and put it in my bag.

Hina is the youngest of three girls. The oldest sister, Kimiko, is thirty-five. She's the same age as me. The next oldest, Erika, is thirty-two. Kimiko is single and works for an Osaka television station. Erika is married and lives abroad. Hina's parents have always been very nice to me. Hina and I have never spoken about getting married, but I can see that her parents would like that for their only daughter still living at home.

"Busy at work, Ryo?" her father asked me the first time we met.

"Yes, it's busy," I replied. "Sometimes we don't have enough staff so it can be a little difficult."

"Are you doing other people's work? It wouldn't surprise me. You're a hard-working man," he said. "My older daughters knew what they wanted to do. Hina lives in a dream world, but now she has you, we don't need to worry."

He was silent a moment, then smiled.

"Please, look after her."

I didn't know what to say, so I just smiled. I'm happy

that they like me, and they think that I'm good for their daughter, but they don't know the real me. They don't know that I want to quit my job and open an antique shop.

When Hina and I get home from the library, I start reading *How Do Worms Work?* I still don't know why Ms. Komachi recommended this book, but I find it very easy to read. Inside the book, I see the leaflet with the photograph of the cat. I take out my smartphone and search online for Cats Now Books and learn that it is in Tokyo. There is an **interview** with the owner, Yasuhara. He is standing in front of the bookshelves holding a black cat and wearing a cat T-shirt. "Lucky man," I think, "living his dream."

I read that Yasuhara also works for a computer business. "Can you do that?" I think. "Work for a business *and* have your own shop?"

Yasuhara says something that interests me. "It is possible to have two **careers** at the same time. One does not have to be more important than the other."

The next day, after work, I visit an antique show. I walk around looking at the beautiful antiques until suddenly I hear my name.

"Ryo? Is that you, Ryo?"

I turn around to see an older man standing behind me. He's wearing a pink jacket with green flowers.

"Mr. Nasuda?" I say after a few seconds.

"Good **memory**!" he shouts.

I knew Mr. Nasuda from the antique shop that I visited

as a child. He was a customer.

"How did you know it was me?" he says. "I look a lot older now, but you haven't changed at all. You still look so worried."

This makes me a little angry, but then I remember that he always said things like that.

"It's been years since I saw you," he continues. "I was sad when the antique shop closed."

"Yes, me too," I reply.

"I remember the police coming to my work," he says.

"The police?" I ask.

I can feel my heart moving faster. All this time, I was worried that Mr. Ebigawa was ill. I didn't think that he might have trouble with the police.

"Yes," Mr. Nasuda says. "Mr. Ebigawa had some money problems, so he ran away."

My heart drops. It's worse than being ill. Now I know that opening a shop can never work. You need money, and when you don't have money bad things happen.

The next day at work is worse than normal. A colleague does not do her work well, and it makes me angry. When I arrive home, Hina is waiting in my apartment and has made dinner. We often spend Friday nights and all of Saturday together. While we are eating, I can't stop thinking about Mr. Ebigawa and my work problems.

"Are you OK, Ryo?" Hina says. "You look worried."

"I'm just busy at work," I say.

"My **online** shop is doing well," she says. "I've sold a lot and the customers are happy."

She is lucky. She can do something that she loves because she still lives at home and doesn't have to worry about money. She doesn't have to do a job that she hates.

"I know it's online, but it feels like a real shop," she continues. "When you have your antique shop—"

"That's easy for you to say," I say, angrily.

She looks surprised. I know that I'm being horrible, but I can't stop.

"I'm not like you, Hina. You don't have to worry if you don't sell anything. It's just a bit of fun for you!"

"It's not a bit of fun!" Hina replies.

I can see that she's angry with me. Maybe I should say sorry, but before I can say anything Hina stands up and walks toward the door.

"I'm going home," she says.

I stay sitting, not moving. I feel bad, but I don't ask her to stay.

With Hina gone, I have nothing to do. I look at my bed and notice the library book *How Do Worms Work?* I begin to read, and I feel a little better. Plants have work to do above and below the ground, but we never see both at the same time. Maybe it's the same with having an office job and owning an antique shop. I think about the interview with Yasuhara and how he has two careers. Is that what Yasuhara is doing?

The next afternoon, I decide to visit Cats Now Books. Inside, lots of cats are walking around. I notice a man

RYO URASE, 35, ACCOUNTANT

wearing a blue shirt. It's Yasuhara.

"Hello," he says, turning toward me. "Can I help you with anything?"

"I came today because I read about you in a leaflet that I found in the Hatori Library."

"Ah, yes. Ms. Komachi recommended us," Yasuhara says, smiling. "Thank you for coming."

Before I can stop myself, I say, "I'm thinking about opening an antique shop. I read your interview about having two careers. I didn't know that it was possible. You work for a business during the week, don't you?"

"That's right," he says.

"Is having two different careers difficult?" I ask.

Yasuhara laughs. "This bookshop was always my dream. My other job makes this dream possible."

I think about the plants working both under and above ground, how we never see both at the same time.

"But aren't you tired?"

"Sometimes. I'm usually here or at my other job. But I love it," he says.

"I want to do what you're doing but I'm not brave enough," I say. "And I don't have time or money."

"The moment you say 'don't' then you're finished," Yasuhara says.

"I don't understand?" I say.

"You have to make 'don't' into something real. Find the money, find the time, become braver," he says, still smiling. "Of course, it's hard work, but my wife helps, and I couldn't

do this without her."

I look at his face and I think of Hina. Both he and Hina are living their dreams, and they are happy.

A few days later, I take the book back to the library and visit Ms. Komachi.

"I went to Cats Now Books," I say.

"Yasuhara is a great friend," Ms. Komachi says, smiling.

"You wanted me to visit that shop, didn't you?" I say.

"I didn't send you there," she says. "You decided to go there. You've already begun."

"Thank you," I say.

After leaving the library, I go to Hina's house to say sorry. When I arrive at her house, she opens the door and asks me to come upstairs to her bedroom.

"I'm sorry," I say, pulling out a bottle and two glasses from my bag.

She looks surprised.

"Well done for selling your sea-glass," I say.

"Thank you," she says. "You think it's a bit of fun, but when I make things with sea-glass I think about the person who might wear it. It's a journey from one person to another and it makes me happy."

I know what she means, and it's why I want my own shop.

"Hina, I have something to tell you," I say. "I'm going to open an antique shop."

"But what about your job?" Hina asks.

"I'm not going to quit. I'm going to keep my job and open the antique shop, too." I want to add, "So, will you help me?" but stop myself. If I say this, she will know that I am asking her to marry me.

"Yes!" Hina says. "And it'll be easier if we do it together. Let's get married as soon as possible."

She says it so easily.

I think about Yasuhara and his wife. This can be me and Hina. I think about how we don't see what is happening below the ground but only what is happening above. It's possible to do two jobs and be happy—one helps the other, and both are important. Finally, *one day* is going to become *tomorrow*.

CHAPTER THREE
Natsumi Sakitani, 40, works in publishing

It's August. For two years, I have worked in **Information Resources** for a **publisher** called Banyusha. Before that, I worked as an **editor** for one of Banyusha's magazines, *Mila*. I was there for thirteen years, and I was doing very well. But then I became **pregnant**.

At that time, I was thirty-seven, so I was happy about being pregnant because I wanted children. But I was also worried about my job. I didn't want people to treat me differently. I was allowed to stay at home with my baby for fourteen months, but I came back just four months later. I wanted to get back to work as soon as possible, so I put three-month-old Futaba in **daycare**.

On my first day back at work, my manager called me into his office.

"Ms. Sakitani, we're **transferring** you to Information Resources," he said.

"Why?" I asked.

"Because it's impossible to work as an editor with a baby," he said. "Information Resources is a nine-to-five job. It's much easier for you."

I was really angry, and I couldn't speak.

Things weren't good at home either. My husband, Shuji, was always at work and couldn't help with the baby much.

I could never make plans. Maybe my manager was right? Maybe being an editor and a mother was impossible?

It's Friday. At five o'clock, I stand up and try not to make any noise. Everybody has their heads down, still working. I'm not doing anything wrong, but I don't like leaving this early. Before having Futaba, I often worked late, and I loved it.

After work, I get Futaba from daycare. Shuji doesn't often get her because he works late. He also works on the weekends. There are so many small jobs that I have to do every evening. Then, on the weekend, I do more housework. Of course, I love Futaba, but looking after a two-year-old child by yourself can be hard.

The next day, Saturday, Shuji leaves for work early. Futaba and I eat breakfast. While she plays with her toys in the living room, I try to do some washing and cleaning. But when I come back, Futaba's toys are all over the floor.

"Fu-*chan*, if you've finished with your toys, let's put them back into the box," I say.

"No!" Futaba shouts.

"I'll give them to someone else if you leave them out."

"NO!"

All the books say that this is normal for a two-year-old child. But it's still difficult not to get angry. Sometimes I think that I'm not good enough to be a mother. Thinking about being alone all weekend with Futaba worries me. I don't know what to do with her. The park is always full of other mothers and their children, and I don't know what to

say to them. Then I remember that the Hatori Library has a play area for children. Maybe we can go there?

"Fu-*chan*, shall we go out?" I say.

Futaba jumps to her feet and smiles.

When we get to the library, we take some books from the shelves and sit down to read in the children's area. Suddenly, a young woman appears.

"Hello, I'm Nozomi," she says. "Do you need any help?"

Futaba points to another book on the shelf.

"That's a great book!" Nozomi says. "Do you want to borrow it?"

"Can we?" I say.

"Yes, anybody who lives in this area can borrow six books for two weeks," Nozomi says. "And if you're looking for anything else, the librarian is in the office."

"I thought that you were the librarian," I say.

"No, I'm training to be one. I am in my first year and still have two more years to study," Nozomi says, smiling.

I remember when I first started at *Mila*, I was as happy as Nozomi is now. I always wanted to work in publishing, so when I joined Banyusha I was very excited. Five years ago, *Mila* **published** stories by the famous writer Mizue Kanata. The readers loved them, and it happened because of me.

Madam Mizue was seventy at the time, and my manager didn't want her to write for *Mila* because the magazine was for younger women. But I knew Madam Mizue's writing, and I knew that her stories would work for the magazine.

NATSUMI SAKITANI, 40, WORKS IN PUBLISHING

At first, Madam Mizue was not interested, but I continued to ask, and she finally said yes. We had a great **relationship**. The stories were loved by the readers, and Banyusha decided to publish them all into one book. This became one of my many jobs. The book even won an **award**. Then, I discovered that I was pregnant.

"Fu-*chan*, shall we ask the librarian about more fun books?" I say.

"I can watch her," Nozomi says. "You can speak with the librarian if you want to."

"Are you sure?" I say.

"It's fine. There's nobody else in here now," Nozomi says.

I see how happy Futuba is with her books, so I walk toward the office and go inside. Behind the desk is a very large woman with white skin. In her hands are some needles that are moving very quickly. She is felting.

As I walk toward her, I notice a box of Honeydome cookies next to her. We had those cookies all the time when I worked at *Mila*.

"What are you looking for?" the librarian says.

"What am I looking for?" I think. I'm looking for so many things, but she doesn't want to hear that.

"Children's books," I say.

I read on her desk that her name is Sayuri Komachi.

"We have many children's books," she says.

"Something for a two-year-old," I say. "But I'm not really sure what children like."

"Having a child is difficult, isn't it?" Ms. Komachi says.

"You can never really know what it's like until you've had one. It's a huge event in your life. I think that people forget how big it is. I also think that being born is the most difficult thing we ever have to do. If you can **survive** that, you can survive anything."

I am silent, I don't know what to say. Here is somebody who seems to understand me.

Ms. Komachi turns back to her computer and begins to type. She then hands me a list of books. The first three books are children's books, but the last one is strange. It's *Door to the Moon* by Yukari Ishii.

I know the name Yukari Ishii because some of my colleagues in *Mila* follow her online. Maybe Yukari Ishii also writes picture books? But then I notice that the book is in a different area in the library than the other ones.

"This is for you. It's a gift," Ms. Komachi says, pulling a felted blue and green globe from her desk. It's the Earth.

"The best thing about felting is that I can change direction even after I've started," she says. "I can change my idea."

"So, it's possible to make something different from what you first wanted to make?" I ask.

Ms. Komachi turns away and says nothing. She isn't interested in talking to me any more. I put the gift into my bag and look for *Door to the Moon*.

When I find the book, I notice how colorful it is. I begin to read and stop at the sentence *The moon is the mother and the wife*. The moon is the mother and the wife? I always thought that the *sun* was the mother because the mother has to be happy and smiling, like the sun. I want to read more, so I take the book with me and go back to find Futaba.

On Monday morning, as I sit down at my desk, I hear someone shout my name. It's Kizawa. She works for *Mila*. She is single and about the same age as me. She looks very tired. After I was transferred, she was given my job and, more importantly, Madam Mizue.

"Can you help me?" she says. "I need to meet Madam Mizue tomorrow, but I have no time. Could you go for me?"

"Yes!" I say, smiling.

Kizawa tells me that the meeting is the next day in a city hotel at 11:00 a.m. I email Madam Mizue and tell her that I'm coming. I'm going to see Madam Mizue!

The next morning, I wake up feeling excited. But Futaba isn't feeling well. Her nose is wet, and her face is hot.

"Is Futaba OK?" Shuji asks. "She doesn't look great."

"I'll take her to daycare," I say. "But if they call, can you pick her up?"

"No, I can't. I'm working late," Shuji says.

I get Futaba ready and take her to daycare. I work at my desk until 10:00 a.m., then just as I'm leaving my smartphone rings. It's Futaba's daycare, and I need to pick her up. "Why is this happening today?" I think.

When I get to Futaba's daycare, I see that she is smiling. She looks fine. Suddenly, I'm crying. "Why is it always the women?" I think. "It is the women who pick up the children from daycare. It is the woman who quits her job."

I send Madam Mizue an email to say sorry and that I cannot come to the meeting.

These things happen with children. We'll meet another time, she replies.

Later that night, Shuji arrives home.

"You're late," I say.

"I was busy," he says.

But he doesn't look tired, and I can smell beer.

"Did you go drinking?" I say, angrily.

"It was just one drink," he says. "Sometimes *you* feel like doing that, don't you?"

"Yes, I do," I shout. "But I can't! I have to take Futaba to daycare, and I have to pick her up. Then I have to make dinner and clean the apartment. And you're never here! I had somewhere that I wanted to go today!"

"I only had one drink!" Shuji shouts back.

"She's your child, too!" I say.

That's when I see Futaba standing at the door.

"Fu-*chan* cleaning," she says, picking up her toys and putting them into her toy box.

She doesn't understand what we're saying, but she knows that it's about her. Then she starts crying. I pick her up and kiss her head. She's the child I wanted. How could I be angry with her? *I'm sorry, Futaba, my beautiful daughter. I'm so sorry.*

The next day, I receive a phone call at work. Madam Mizue is downstairs and wants to see me. I go downstairs to see her and smile. I wanted to see her so much! But then I start crying.

"Let's get some lunch," she says, touching my arm.

Madam Mizue is here to see Kizawa because they want to make a movie about her stories. I'm jealous that Kizawa is doing this. They were the stories that I worked so hard on.

"It wasn't easy writing those stories," Madam Mizue says as she eats.

"Really?" I reply, surprised.

"I was so worried all the time. I thought I was too old for the young women reading them. But I loved writing them," she says, smiling. "It was because of you, Ms. Sakitani. You were there when the stories were born. We did it together. You were the mother and father for me."

"I was worried that I would never see you again," I say, crying again. "I'm so jealous of Kizawa. I keep thinking that my life is not how I want it to be because of my daughter. I hate myself for thinking it."

The memory of Futaba picking up her toys and putting them away makes me sad.

Madam Mizue puts down her coffee. "What you're feeling is very normal. If you're single, you are jealous of people who are married with children. If you're married with children, you are jealous of people who are single. But nothing is better or worse."

"Thank you," I say.

For the first time in a long time, I feel happy.

The next evening, when Futaba is sleeping, I decide to read *Door to the Moon*. *The heart has two eyes*, it says, *one is the sun eye and the other is the moon eye*.

I think about Ms. Komachi and her gift. "What do I want to do now? Where do I want to go?" I think about Madam Mizue and being the mother and father to her stories. Suddenly, I know what I want. I want to be a **fiction** editor and work with writers like Madam Mizue. I want to help writers make their stories as good as possible.

The next weekend, Shuji stays with Futaba at home. He understands now that he needs to help me more.

I decide to go to the library, but first I need to buy some new glasses, so I go to Eden. I am surprised to see a new person working here.

"Kiriyama!" I say as I enter.

I know Kiriyama from working at *Mila*.

"Ms. Sakitani?" Kiriyama replies, surprised.

"What are you doing here?" I ask.

"I quit the magazine," he says. "I started here last month."

It's nice to see him. He looks healthy and very happy. He was very thin when he worked on the magazine, and I worried about him sometimes.

"I'm thinking of changing jobs, too," I say, suddenly. "I want to work in fiction publishing."

"I actually know someone who works for Maple Publications. Are you interested?" Kiriyama says.

"Maple Publications?" I say. "They publish children's books, don't they?"

"Yes. My friend is retiring so they need someone. If you want, I can help you get an interview?"

"But I'm forty, and I have a two-year-old child," I say.

"They publish children's books," Kiriyama says. "It's good that you have a child."

"Kiriyama, why are you doing this for me?" I say. I am not his friend, and he doesn't need to help me. He is just someone that I worked with.

"You were very good at your job," he says. "And you want to publish good books. We all want to read good books."

I leave Eden smiling and go to the library to speak with Ms. Komachi.

"Thank you for your help the other day. I loved *Door to the Moon*," I say.

"I'm happy to hear that," Ms. Komachi says.

"Yes. It's changed my life," I reply.

"You say that it's the book, but sometimes it's *how* you read the book," she says.

Later, when I'm working at Maple, I learn something important. When we read, we use our moon eye. But when we **edit**, we use our sun eye. Both are important.

This is what I want to do. I want to make fiction that helps people understand themselves better, while looking down at an open page.

CHAPTER FOUR
Hiroya Suda, 30, not working

When I was a child, my friends were from the past and the future, and sometimes they were from other worlds. They were more real to me than my classmates. I never got bored when I was with them. So, what happened? I'm embarrassed to say that I reached thirty without becoming anything at all.

It's Friday, and I'm sitting on the sofa. Mom puts her bag of vegetables and fruit on the kitchen table.

"I forgot to buy bananas," she says. "Oh, and some other vegetables, too. But I must get ready for work now."

I say nothing but I know that she wants me to go back to the market.

"Hiroya, would you go back for me?"

"OK," I say.

The market isn't far from where I live. It's near a library, but I've never been there. Mom sometimes goes. I stand up, go to the front door, and walk toward the market. When I get there, I find the vegetables and bananas and pay for them. I'm about to leave when I notice something on the table.

"Monger!" I shout.

It is a Monger toy, a character from the Fujiko F. Fujio **manga** books. Monger is round and has a strange head.

I reach out to touch it, but the woman who sold me the bananas stops me.

"Sorry, you can't buy that. It's one of Sayuri's felted gifts."

"Sayuri?" I reply.

"Sayuri Komachi. She works in the library. She makes them."

"Monger is not very famous, so this girl sounds interesting," I think. "What's she like?" I decide to go to the library to see if I can find her. When I arrive, a young woman is standing in front of some books. She's very beautiful, and I start smiling. But then I feel stupid.

"Hello," the young woman says.

"Hi," I say quietly. "Does this library have any manga?"

"Yes, we do," she says, smiling back at me.

"Was it you who felted the Monger?" I ask, suddenly. "I saw it outside with the lady who sells the bananas."

"Ah no, I'm Nozomi. Ms. Komachi the librarian made that. She's in the office. You can talk to her if you want. She can also recommend some manga."

"Thank you," I say.

I walk toward the office and go inside. Wow! This woman is huge! My heart stops. I look at her for a moment and see that she is holding some needles and felting something. This must be Sayuri Komachi.

As I'm looking at her, she stops what she's doing and turns to me.

"What are you looking for?" she says.

"What am I looking for?" I think.

"I don't know what I'm looking for," I say. And suddenly I have begun to cry.

"Rumiko Takahashi is good, don't you think?" she says.

Is she talking about manga? She heard me speaking to Nozomi.

"Um, yes," I reply.

"*Urusei Yatsura* and *Maison Ikkoku* are good, too."

"Yes!"

We start talking about our favorite manga. Ms. Komachi knows everyone and everything. As she talks, I notice an orange box on her desk. I know that box — it's a Honeydome cookie box. My grandma gave them to me as a child. Ms. Komachi opens the box and puts her needles inside. There are no cookies in there any more.

"How do you know so much about manga?" she says.

"I read it a lot as a child," I say.

When I was little, I read a lot. That's how I met my friends—they were manga. Then I started drawing them, and I couldn't stop. After high school, I went to art school. But after that, I couldn't find a job. My art was a little strange and nobody liked it. I'm not good at anything else. So here I am, thirty years old, with no job and still living with my mother.

"I love manga artists. I studied them at art school, but I wasn't good enough," I say.

"Why is that?" Ms. Komachi says.

"You have to be very good. Only one in one hundred people can be an artist," I say.

"You can be that one," she says.

"What?" I say.

She turns to her computer and begins to type. She then hands me a piece of paper with one book on it. A book called ***Evolution***.

"This is also for you," she says reaching into her desk. "It's a gift."

"It's a felted plane," I say. "I don't understand."

Ms. Komachi doesn't say anything. I don't think that she wants to talk to me any more, so I take the plane and the

HIROYA SUDA, 30, NOT WORKING

paper and try to find the book.

When I find it, I see that it's large and very heavy. It's full of colorful photographs of birds, plants, and animals that look like manga drawings. This is so strange. I don't know why Ms. Komachi recommended this book, but I like it. I really like it.

"Do you want to borrow it?" Nozomi calls out to me.

"Oh, I don't know. It's too heavy to take home."

"You can read it here," Ms. Komachi calls from the office. "I will keep it under my desk for you."

I start crying again. It's OK. It's OK for me to be here.

The next day is Saturday, and I have to go to my old high school. It's been many years since I left, and I don't want to go back. I felt **invisible** at school. But I have to go because they are going to open a **time capsule** that was put into the ground on the day that we finished school. Inside the time capsule were the future dreams that we all wrote for ourselves. I don't want anybody to see what is written on mine, so I have to go and get it. But I won't go to the party after it.

In my last year of high school, I thought that I was going to be a famous artist. I think that's what I wrote for the time capsule. But now, here I am back at school again, without a job.

I can see a crowd of people standing under a large tree where we put the time capsule. I hear somebody shout my name. It's Seitaro. We weren't good friends, but we talked sometimes. He was quiet, and he was always reading. After we finished school, we sent each other New Year's cards. That's how I know that he went to university and then got a job at an office.

"You look well," Seitaro says.

"You too," I say, hoping he doesn't ask me about work.

"OK, we're all here now," comes a voice from behind us. It's my old teacher.

"Let's start," he says, opening the time capsule.

We all watch as he reaches inside, pulling out pieces of paper. He then hands them to the people standing in the crowd. Everybody is happy and smiling and having a great time. They have lives, jobs, and families—not like me. Finally, my name is called. I take the piece of paper and put it into my jacket pocket. I don't want to look at it.

Seitaro takes his paper and reads it to me, "*I will become a writer*," he says.

"Did you?" I say.

"I wrote a book," he says.

"When was it published?" I ask.

"It hasn't been published yet," he says. "You went to design school, didn't you?"

"Yes," I say, "but my drawings were too strange. Nobody liked them."

"I'm the opposite. People always say that my writing is boring."

"But you keep writing?" I say.

"Yes, when I'm not working in the office," he says.

"I worry that I'm too old to be published, but other writers were first published when they were forty or fifty. Everybody has their own journey that works best for them."

He's still following his dream. I like that about Seitaro.

I walk toward the office and find *Evolution* on Ms. Komachi's desk. I take it to the table and open it. I turn to a page about Charles Darwin and Alfred Wallace. It's about evolution and how animals **adapt** to their environment to survive. I learned about this at school. Those that don't adapt die. That's the idea.

I've never heard of Wallace. When people think of evolution, they usually think of Darwin. But Wallace had the same ideas and also wrote about them. Wallace published first, but everybody remembers Darwin. I don't like this. The same thing happened to me at art school. There was a boy in my class who always **copied** my drawings. The teachers loved his work because he was a better artist than me. But the drawings were my idea. The book makes me sad. Then I see a photo of a dead bird—it's again sad but also beautiful. It's called a *Confuciusornis*, and it lived millions of years ago. I suddenly want to draw it. I haven't felt like this in a long time.

I borrow a pen and some paper from Nozomi. I look at the *Confuciusornis* and study everything that I can see. Then, slowly, I start to draw a picture. I draw for a while, adding things as I go.

"Wow!" Nozomi shouts, coming up behind me. "I've

never seen anything like that before."

"Thank you," I say. "My drawings are usually too dark and strange for most people."

"But some people *love* dark and strange. Can I have it?" she asks.

I don't know what to say. "Somebody likes my pictures," I think.

On my way home, I feel very excited. But, when I open the door, I hear that Mom is on the phone. I know who she is speaking to because she sounds happy. My heart drops.

"Your brother's moving back to Japan in April!" she says, putting the phone down.

"Oh nice," I say, walking toward the bathroom so she won't see me cry.

I think about *Evolution* and adapting to survive. After our dad left, my big brother was always angry with me. He hates me. He's always been the cleverer one, even at school. After he went to university, he got a good career and gave Mom some money. Four years ago, he went to work in Germany, and I was happy. But now he's coming back.

I remember the plane that Ms. Komachi gave me. I'll never build a plane or be able to fly.

What are you looking for? When Ms. Komachi asked me this question, I thought, "I'm still looking for a place where I can be who I am."

Suddenly, my smartphone rings. It's Seitaro.

"I'm going to be published!" he shouts. "I got an email from an editor, Ms. Sakitani. She liked my writing and wanted to meet me. We met a few times and now it's going to be published!"

"That's great!" I say, smiling.

Seitaro's dream is coming true.

I don't know what to do, so I go back outside and walk. I put my hands into my jacket pocket and find the piece of paper from the time capsule. I open it: *I will draw art that people will remember.*

Did I really write that? That was my ambition! I was sure it was *I'm going to be a famous artist* but it wasn't. I remember Nozomi asking me for my drawing. She liked it, and she wanted it. Maybe it's not too late.

The next day, I go back to the library. I take *Evolution* and sit down at the table. I choose some more pictures and begin to draw them. As I'm drawing, I can hear Ms. Komachi talking with Nozomi at her desk.

"Can you help with the office cleaning?" Ms. Komachi asks. "Our cleaner is having a baby, so she's leaving soon."

Nozomi nods but doesn't look very happy.

I stand up.

"I could do it," I say, without thinking.

Ms. Komachi turns around, looks at me for a long time, and then smiles.

In the beginning, it was difficult to get here in the morning. In the past, I stayed up late and woke up late, but after a few weeks, it was fine. Then, Ms. Komachi began telling people that I could draw. People started asking me to draw things for them, or their children.

At the library, I feel useful. I have ambition. I have somewhere to be. When I first got paid, I gave it all to Mom, who gave it back to me and cried. I wanted to say sorry and to say thank you. She always tried to help me, even when I was doing nothing. When my brother comes back, I'm sure that won't change. I will go with Mom to meet him at the airport.

Ms. Komachi has taught me something important. In the long history of evolution, I'm living now, in the present.

CHAPTER FIVE
Masao Gonno, 65, retired

I became sixty-five on the last day of September. After forty-two years, it was also my last day of work, I was **retiring**. I was the manager at an office. I did not do great things, but I did not make big mistakes either. I was just a manager.

On the day I left, I was given some flowers and a "thank you" for my hard work. I was happy to leave. I took one last look at the office and thought, "What am I going to do now?"

When my daughter, Chie, was young, I was always too busy to spend the weekends with her. She is an adult now and has her own apartment.

In the six months since I left my job, I have learned three things. One is that sixty-five is not as old as I thought. This was a surprise. Second, I have nothing to do. I like drinking a beer in the evening and watching television on Sunday evening, but I'm not excited about anything. The third thing is that now I don't have a job, I'm invisible. Talking to people was a big part of my day. When I left, I noticed that all my relationships were with my colleagues. I had no real friends.

I'm sitting in front of the television when my wife, Yoriko, arrives home from work.

"Did you bring in the clothes from outside?" she asks.

"Sorry," I say. "I forgot."

She smiles, steps outside and hands me the clothes through

the door. When Yoriko asks me to do something, I always forget. I'm not sure how to do housework, but Yoriko never gets angry at me.

"I got you this," she says today, pulling a piece of paper from her bag. It has *GO CLASS* written at the top. "It's for a *Go* class at the library."

Yoriko teaches a computer class at the library every Wednesday. She's very good, and her students love her.

"I've never played it," I say.

"It'll be good for you," she says.

So, Yoriko thinks that I should play *Go*. About twenty years ago, I decided to learn English. It was difficult, and I remember thinking that, after forty, it was too late to learn anything, and I quit. So maybe learning *Go* will be a good thing.

On Monday morning, I go to the library and find the class. There are a few people there already. An old man sitting at the back calls out to me.

"Mr. Gonno! Your wife has told me about you," he says, smiling. "I'm Mr. Yakita."

"Thank you for letting me join your class," I say.

It feels strange talking with someone about something that isn't my job. He invites me to sit down with him and explains how to play *Go*. I listen carefully.

"Your wife is wonderful," he says, suddenly. "I'm jealous of you. She's funny and intelligent. I'm **divorced**. A lot of people **divorce** after retiring. You don't leave the house to go to work any more, so you're both home all day."

WHAT YOU ARE LOOKING FOR IS IN THE LIBRARY

"This man likes to talk," I think. I don't know what to say so I just smile.

"Even my clothes made my wife angry," Mr. Yakita says. "I was surprised when it happened, but I think divorcing was the best thing to do."

After the class, I am still unsure about how to play *Go*, maybe because Mr. Yakita kept speaking about his **divorce**. I decide to check the library and walk toward a young girl who is holding some books.

"Hello," I say. "Do you have any books about *Go*?"

The young girl smiles at me and points toward the office on the other side of the room.

"My name is Nozomi but if you need any recommendations, the librarian is in the office. Her name is Sayuri Komachi."

I smile back and enter the office. Then I stop. A very large woman is sitting behind a desk. She is busy doing something with her hands, which continue to move without stopping. When I look closer, I can see that she is felting. Next to her is an orange box. It's a Honeydome cookie box made by Kuremiyado—the place where I worked for so many years.

"What are you looking for?" the librarian says, looking up quickly.

"What am I looking for?" I think. "A new way to live?"

"I would like a book about *Go*. I tried it for the first time today," I reply.

Ms. Komachi puts the felting needles into the cookie box.

"*Go* is a very interesting game," she says. "Each game makes you think about life and death."

"That doesn't sound fun," I think. "I thought games were fun."

"Maybe it's not the right game for me then," I say. Then I point at the cookie box, trying to change the topic. "Do you like these?" I ask. "They're Kuremiyado cookies. I worked there until I retired."

Ms. Komachi's eyes open wide, and she begins smiling.

"Thank you!" she says. "Thank you for these wonderful cookies!"

"That's nice of you to say, but I don't work for Kuremiyado any more," I say, sadly. "I feel like retiring from my job has been the same as retiring from life. When I was working,

I wanted more time for life. Now that I have time, I don't know what to do with it."

I didn't mean to say all of that, but I feel able to tell this huge, warm woman what I'm really feeling.

Ms. Komachi turns to her computer, begins typing, and then hands me a list of books. Most are about playing *Go*, but the last one is called **Frogs** *and Others* by Shinpei Kusano. Before I can ask why it's on the list, Ms. Komachi reaches into her desk and pulls out a felted red crab.

"It's a free gift," she says.

"OK," I say, but I don't really understand.

After dinner that evening, I look at the books that I borrowed from the library. First, I look at the books about *Go*. I know that I wanted them, but they are boring. The book that I find interesting is *Frogs and Others*. On the front is a picture of three frogs sitting by the river. I turn the pages until I find something about **poetry**. The writer recommends copying poetry so you can enter the life of the **poet**. Then he recommends writing your own poetry. This makes me laugh. I could never do that. But I can copy someone else's poetry, and it's easier than learning *Go*.

I take some paper and find the poem "Song of Spring", which is about a frog. Then, I copy it on to the paper with my pen. I don't understand the poem very much, but I'm enjoying what I'm doing. Maybe it *is* more difficult than learning *Go*.

The next afternoon, Yoriko and I go to a store called Eden because Yoriko knows a student from her computer class who works there. When we arrive, we find Tomoka, who is very happy to see us. She looks around twenty years old and seems to really enjoy her job.

"Your wife has helped me so much," Tomoka says as Yoriko tries on some clothes.

"I don't think that *I* help her very much," I reply. "Since I retired, I'm always home and wear indoor clothes all the time. I can't even cook." And suddenly, I think about Mr. Yakita and divorce.

Tomoka thinks for a few seconds and then, with a big smile, she says, "Why don't you try making rice balls?"

"Rice balls?" I say. "Do you think my wife would like that?"

"Yes," Tomoka says, still smiling.

"Is that because your boyfriend made you rice balls?" I ask.

Tomoka's face turns bright red.

Suddenly, Yoriko's phone rings.

"It's Chie," she says, coming back to us. "She has that book that I want."

We say goodbye to Tomoka, and we walk back to the car. Chie works at Meishin Books. Chie walks toward us when we arrive and points to lots of cards and books on the shelves.

"I made that display," she says.

"It looks great," Yoriko says.

"Thank you," Chie replies. "It's really important and helps sell more books."

"She really loves her job," I think.

"You came to get the book, right?" Chie says to Yoriko.

"Yes, and I want some magazines, too," Yoriko says as she walks toward a different area of the shop.

"Where are your poetry books?" I ask Chie, suddenly, without thinking.

Chie's eyes grow wide. "Poetry books? By who?"

"Shinpei Kusano," I say.

"I like him, too," she says. "There was one poem about a frog."

"'Song of Spring'?" I say.

"Yes, that's it. Well done, Dad," she says.

"I don't understand his poems much," I say.

"You don't have to worry about understanding poetry," Chie says. "Just enjoy the feeling or the sound of the poem as you read it."

Yoriko arrives back. "This looks great," she says, holding up a magazine. "I want the gift that comes with it."

I remember the gift that Ms. Komachi gave me, and I pull it out of my jacket pocket.

"A crab!" Chie shouts.

"Would you like it?" I say.

She takes it in her hand, looking pleased. I smile. If a felted crab can make her happy, then she is still a child.

After we arrive home, I read the poem "The Song of Spring" again. I still don't understand everything, but I'm enjoying the feeling and the sound of the poem.

Then I start reading one called "Window" which is quite long. I read the lines, *waves draw close, waves pull back, waves draw close, waves pull back.*

If the poem is called "Window", why is it talking about waves? I copy the poem on to some paper and read it again and again.

The next day, a box arrives full of flowers from Yoriko's family.

"These are lovely," Yoriko says. "Let's give some of them to Mr. Ebigawa to thank him for helping me with my bike yesterday."

Mr. Ebigawa is the manager of the building that we live in. He looks after the apartments and anything that is broken.

I pick up the flowers and walk toward his office. The manager's office is larger than it looks from the outside. I can see Mr. Ebigawa through a large window. *A window?* I think about the poem. Mr. Ebigawa is watching something on a computer, but he looks up when I call his name. He opens the door, and I hold the bag of flowers out to him.

"Please, have these," I say. "To say thanks for the bike."

"Thank you," Mr. Ebigawa replies. "Why don't you come in?"

I like Mr. Ebigawa and think that he is an interesting man. I don't know him very well, but he always wears the same hat every day. I ask him about his job, and he tells me some things about being a building manager. As he speaks, I see people coming in and out through the large window. *Window, waves draw close, waves pull back.* Day after day, people are coming and going.

"I'm **retired**," I say. "I did the same job for so many years, and now I do nothing."

"I've had many different jobs," Mr. Ebigawa says. "I was a cleaner, and I worked in an office. I had a bicycle shop,

MASAO GONNO, 65, RETIRED

and I also had an antique shop."

"An antique shop?" I say.

Mr. Ebigawa smiles. "I didn't make any money, but I enjoyed it. I had to close the shop because someone who I borrowed money from thought that I couldn't pay them back. The police asked me a lot of questions and my customers stopped coming."

I shake my head.

"But the police were just doing their job," Mr. Ebigawa continues. "And I didn't tell my customers what was happening."

I stop shaking my head. He's right.

"It was sad, but there was a high-school student who often came to the shop. He's now opening his own antique shop. My shop didn't work but it's great that it **inspired** someone else."

I look down at the ground.

"I've never inspired anybody," I say.

Mr. Ebigawa looks into my eyes. "This is how I see it, Mr. Gonno. Everybody has a place in the world."

I don't really know what to say, but it's true. "*Waves draw close, waves pull back*," I think. People are coming and going.

The next day, I visit Meishin Books and see Chie holding some books. When I call out to her, she smiles.

"What's this?" I say, pointing to a sign behind her. "Did you make that, too?"

"Yes. It's for *The Pink Plane Tree* by Mizue Kanata. It's a great book. It's going to be a movie," she says.

She always looks so happy when she's talking about books.

"Did you want to look at some more poetry?" she asks.

"No, I just wanted to ask you something," I reply. "I hear books aren't selling that well any more, and that they are disappearing. Is that true?"

"No! Stop it. Bookshops and books will always be necessary. People need them. I'll never allow them to disappear from the world," Chie says.

"I'm sorry, I know you care about your work. You're better than me," I say. "I never did anything important."

She shakes her head. "Dad, you worked in the same place all your life. That's great. Everybody loves Kuremiyado cookies."

I remember Ms. Komachi saying the same thing.

"But I didn't make them," I reply.

"I've never sold a book that I've written myself," Chie replies. "But I can sell a book that I think is good. It isn't enough to have one person writing something. Many people help to publish a book, and I'm happy to be one of them."

Chie and I have never talked about work like this before. When did she become an adult?

I didn't make the cookies. But like Chie, I believed in them and worked hard to sell them. I had a place. This thought makes those forty-two years seem OK.

"I just remembered," she says reaching into her bag, "I love that you're reading Shinpei Kusano, so I bought it."

Chie pulls out *Frogs and Others* and looks through the pages, stopping at one poem.

"I really like this poem. It's called 'Window'. I think that it's different from the others."

I'm pleased to know that we like the same poem.

"I don't understand why it's called 'Window'," I say.

"In my mind, he's at a hotel, and when he opens the window, he can see the sea. Maybe before he could only see the room, and it was his first time seeing the sea after opening the window. It's like he suddenly discovered a world outside waiting for him."

Chie sees the poem differently from me. Her understanding is more positive. Only Shinpei Kusano knows what he actually saw. But each reader can have their own understanding, which is a good thing.

When Chie puts the book into her bag, I see the felted crab and smile.

"I love it," she says, seeing my face. "Do you remember doing the crab race together when I was in school?"

"The crab race?" I ask.

"You don't remember?" she says, laughing. "It was a race for parents and children. We had to walk to the side, like a crab. We finished last."

"Yes, now I remember. We did," I say, laughing too.

"You said that walking like a crab makes the world look bigger and wider," Chie says. "So now when I don't know what to do, I try to see the world like a crab."

I feel like I'm about to cry. For so long I've worried about my relationship with Chie and how I was always working and not spending time with her as a child. But life is not a straight journey. It is much wider than you think.

A few days later, I go back to the library. I walk toward the office and find Ms. Komachi felting. She stops when she notices me and looks at the paper bag in my hands. It has Kuremiyado written on it.

"I brought you a gift," I say.

"Thank you very much!" Ms. Komachi says, taking the cookies from me.

"Can I ask something?" I say. "How do you choose the gifts that you make?"

"**Inspiration**," she says.

"I don't understand."

"People find their own meaning in the gifts," Ms. Komachi says. "It's the same with books. Readers understand things differently."

I know now that every day is as important as the next day and that everybody has their own place in the world.

On a sunny afternoon, I meet Yoriko at the library. She's teaching in the morning, and we are going to have some lunch after her class.

We sit down together in the park, and I show her the rice balls that I have made for her. Yoriko is very surprised when she sees them. Seeing her face makes me happy, too.

I have a list of things that I want to try now. I want to cook more, I want to learn English, I even want to try felting. I plan to enjoy every day and look at the world in a wider way—like a crab.

MASAO GONNO, 65, RETIRED

During-reading questions

CHAPTER ONE

1 Why won't Tomoka tell Saya that she works in a clothes shop?
2 What did Kiriyama do before working in the glasses shop?
3 When is the computer class?
4 Tomoka says, "For the first time in a long while, I feel a little excited about something." What does she mean, do you think?
5 What's inside the orange box on Sayuri Komachi's desk?
6 Why does Sayuri Komachi give Tomoka a felted frying pan, do you think?
7 Why did Kiriyama quit his old job?

CHAPTER TWO

1 Ryo says, "It all began with a spoon ..." What does he mean, do you think?
2 What did Mr. Ebigawa and the other customers teach Ryo?
3 What is Hina doing when Ryo first meets her?
4 Why do Ryo and Hina go to the library?
5 Sayuri Komachi tells Ryo to look at the leaflets before he leaves the library. Why does she do this, do you think?
6 What happened to Mr. Ebigawa?
7 Yasuhara says. "The moment you say 'don't' then you're finished." What does he mean, do you think?

CHAPTER THREE

1. Why is Natsumi worried about her job after becoming pregnant?
2. Why didn't the manager **not** want Madam Mizue to write for *Mila*?
3. Natsumi says, "Why is it always the women?" What does she mean, do you think?
4. How does Kiriyama help Natsumi with her job?
5. Natsumi thinks the book has changed her life. Sayuri Komachi tells Natsumi, "You say that it's the book, but sometimes it's *how* you read the book." What does she mean, do you think?

CHAPTER FOUR

1. Hiroya says, "When I was a child, my friends were from the past and the future, and sometimes they were from other worlds." What does he mean, do you think?
2. Why does Hiroya go to the library?
3. Why does Hiroya like the book that Sayuri Komachi recommends?
4. How does Hiroya feel about going back to school?
5. Who is moving back to Japan?
6. What is Hiroya's job at the library?

CHAPTER FIVE

1 Why is the last day of September important for Masao?
2 Why did Masao stop learning English?
3 Masao says, "I feel like retiring from my job has been the same as retiring from life." What does he mean, do you think?
4 Why does Tomoka's face turn bright red?
5 Masao and Chie each read the poem differently. What does this teach Masao?
6 What does Sayuri Komachi say about the gifts that she makes? What does she mean, do you think?

After-reading questions

1 How are the main people in the five stories connected?
2 How does each person change in the story, do you think?
3 What have you learned about Japan that you didn't know before?
4 Why do you think the book is called *What You Are Looking For Is In The Library*?

Exercises

CHAPTER ONE

1) Write the correct question word. Then answer the questions in your notebook.

1 ...*Whose*... boyfriend is a doctor?
2 .... long has Tomoka worked at Eden?
3 .... is Mrs. Numauchi?
4 .... does Tomoka get her lunch?
5 .... does Tomoka want to change jobs?

CHAPTER TWO

2) Complete these sentences in your notebook, using the names from the box.

Mr. Taguchi	Hina	Mr. Nasuda
Yasuhara	Nozomi	Morinaga

1 ...*Mr. Taguchi*... finds things difficult to understand.
2 .... is still training.
3 .... is sad that the antique shop closed.
4 .... has an online business.
5 .... has two jobs.

CHAPTER THREE

3) **Match the two parts of these sentences in your notebook.**

Example: *1 – d*

1 "Ms. Sakitani, we're transferring
2 Then, on the weekend,
3 All the books say that
4 I remember when I first started at *Mila*,
5 The book
6 We had those cookies all the time
7 I'm looking for so many things,

a I was as happy as Nozomi is now.
b even won an award.
c this is normal for a two-year-old child.
d you to Information Resources."
e but she doesn't want to hear that.
f when I worked at *Mila*.
g I do more housework.

CHAPTER FOUR

4 **Put the words in the correct order to make sentences in your notebook.**

1 Friday, It's sofa. on sitting and the I'm
It's Friday, and I'm sitting on the sofa.
2 from a was It character the books. manga
3 do manga? about much know so you How
4 school. I felt at invisible
5 go after the won't But to I party it.
6 jacket I paper it take pocket. the piece and put of into my

CHAPTER FIVE

5 **Choose the correct adjective to complete these sentences in your notebook.**

1 The third thing is that now I don't have a job, I'm *invisible* / **awake**.
2 It was too late to learn anything, and I **quit / end**.
3 She's funny and intelligent. I'm **married / divorced**.
4 I feel able to tell this huge, **hot / warm** woman what I'm really feeling.
5 I know that I wanted them, but they are **sad / boring**.
6 I can copy someone else's poetry, and it's **easier / more difficult** than learning *Go*.

Project work

1. Choose one of the following and write a diary page about it.
   - Tomoka Fujiki makes castella, just like in *Guri and Gura*.
   - Ryo meets Hina on the beach.
   - Hiroya's first day working at the library.

2. Write about how libraries have changed in your country in the last twenty years.

3. Write a review of this book. Did you like it? Why/Why not?

4. What do you think happens to Ryo and Hina after the story? Think about their dreams and their jobs. What do you think they are doing? Write another chapter, five years in the future.

An answer key for all questions and exercises can be found at **www.penguinreaders.co.uk**

Glossary

adapt (v.)
If you *adapt* to a new or different thing, you change what you do because of it.

ambition (n.)
something that you very much want to do in your life

award (n.)
a thing that you win because you have done something very special

career (n.)
the most important job or jobs that you do through your life

colleague (n.)
a person who you work with

copy (v.)
If you *copy* something, you make a thing that looks the same.

customer (n.)
a person who buys things in a shop or from a business

daycare (n.)
a place that looks after young children during the day, usually because their mothers or fathers are at work

divorce (v. and n.); **divorced** (adj.)
When people who are married decide not to be married any more, then they are *divorced*. *Divorce* is the noun of *divorce*.

edit (v.); **editor** (n.)
To *edit* a piece of writing is to read and make changes to it. An *editor* is a person who works on books, *magazines* or newspapers.

embarrassed (adj.)
feeling worried about what other people think about you or something that you have done

evolution (n.)
the way that living things slowly change and *adapt* to changes in the world, over millions of years

felt (n. and v.); **felted** (adj.)
Felt is a thick, soft and used to make clothes or toys. A *felted* thing is made of *felt*.

fiction (n.)
stories about people or events that are not real

frog (n.)
a small green animal with big eyes and long legs for jumping. *Frogs* live near water.

frying pan (n.)
a flat round metal thing that you use for frying (= cooking in hot oil or butter)

Information Resources (n.)
a part of a business that works with information that the business needs

inspire (v.); **inspiration** (n.)
To *inspire* someone is to make them want to do something and feel that they are able to do it. *Inspiration* is when a thing or person gives you new ideas or *inspires* you to do something.

interview (n.)
when you ask someone questions to learn information about them, sometimes to decide if they will get a job

invisible (adj.)
If a person or thing is *invisible*, no one can see them.

leaflet (n.)
a piece of paper that gives information about something

librarian (n.)
a person who works in a library

list (n.)
words, names or numbers that have been written one below the other

magazine (n.)
a thin book with large pages and pictures. You can buy a new *magazine* every week or month.

manager (n.)
a person whose job is to decide what work other people must do and tell them to do it

manga (n.)
Japanese books that tell stories through drawings

memory (n.)
1) how you are able to remember things. A person can have a good or bad *memory*.
2) something that you remember from the past

needle (n.)
a very thin piece of metal that is used) for making clothes, or for *felting*

online (adv. and adj.)
on the internet

personality (n.)
Your *personality* is the way that you do things and what you usually think, say, like, etc.

pocket (n.)
a place in trousers, a coat, etc. where you can put things

poet (n.); **poetry** (n.)
A *poet* writes poems. *Poetry* is poems, or the writing of poems.

pregnant (adj.)
A *pregnant* person has a baby growing inside their body.

publish (v.); **publishing** (n.); **publisher** (n.)
To *publish* a piece of writing is to put it in a place where people can read it, for example in books, *magazines*, or newspapers. *Publishing* is the business of making and selling books and *magazines*. A *publisher* is a person or business that makes and sells books and *magazines*.

quit (v.)
to leave your job, school, university, etc.

recipe (n.)
information about how to make a cake or meal. *Recipes* are *published* in books or *magazines*, or *online*.

recommend (v.); **recommendation** (n.)
1) to say that something or someone is good
2) to tell someone that you think it is a good idea for them to do something. *Recommendation* is the noun of *recommend*.

relationship (n.)
You like a person and they like you. You and this person have a good *relationship*.

retire (v.); **retired** (adj.)
to stop working, usually because you are old. *Retired* is the adjective of *retire*.

skill (n.)
a thing that you have learned to do well

staff (n.)
the people who work for a person or business

survive (v.)
to not die after a dangerous or difficult thing

time capsule (n.)
You put things or information from the time you are living in into a *time capsule*. It is put into the ground for people in the future to discover.

transfer (v.)
to move someone or something from one place, job, school, etc. to another

type (v.)
to write something by pressing parts of a computer, mobile phone, etc. with your fingers

Penguin 🐧 Readers

Visit **www.penguinreaders.co.uk**
for FREE Penguin Readers resources
and digital and audio versions of this book.